Vietnamese Heritage
Celebrating Diversity in My Classroom

By Tamra B. Orr

SOUTH HUNTINGTON PUB. LIB.
145 PIDGEGON HILL ROAD
HUNTINGTON STA., NY 11746

21st Century Junior Library

Published in the United States of America by
Cherry Lake Publishing
Ann Arbor, Michigan
www.cherrylakepublishing.com

Reading Adviser: Marla Conn MS, Ed., Literacy specialist, Read-Ability, Inc.

Photo Credits: © Nerea Urdampilleta / Shutterstock Images, cover; © buimaithien / Shutterstock Images, 4; © Steve Lovegrove / Shutterstock Images, 6; © nikitabuida / Shutterstock Images, 8; © sonyworld / Shutterstock Images, 10; © steve estvanik / Shutterstock Images, 12; © Vietnam Stock Images / Shutterstock Images, 14; © Ohm2499 / Shutterstock Images, 16; © FeyginFoto / Shutterstock Images, 18; © Saigonese Photographer / Shutterstock Images, 20

Library of Congress Cataloging-in-Publication Data
Name: Orr, Tamra, author.
Title: Vietnamese heritage / by Tamra B. Orr.
Description: Ann Arbor : Cherry Lake Publishing, 2018. | Series: Celebrating diversity in my classroom | Includes bibliographical references and index.
Identifiers: LCCN 2017036241 | ISBN 9781534107397 (hardcover) | ISBN 9781534109377 (pdf) | ISBN 9781534108387 (pbk.) | ISBN 9781534120365 (hosted ebook)
Subjects: LCSH: Vietnam—Social life and customs—Juvenile literature.
Classification: LCC DS556.42 .O77 2018 | DDC 959.7—dc23
LC record available at https://lccn.loc.gov/2017036241

Cherry Lake Publishing would like to acknowledge the work of The Partnership for 21st Century Skills.
Please visit *www.p21.org* for more information.

Printed in the United States of America
Corporate Graphics

CONTENTS

5 **Vibrant Vietnam**

7 *Han Hanh Gap Ong!*

11 *Following Cao Dai*

15 *Pho and Street Food*

19 *Gia Dinh and Xe May*

22 Glossary

23 Find Out More

24 Index

24 About the Author

The city of Hoi An in central Vietnam has been inhabited by humans for more than 2,000 years.

Vibrant Vietnam

Vietnam is an S-shaped country bordered by the South China Sea.

Vietnam is only about the size of New Mexico. Yet more than 93 million people live there. Most live in Hanoi in the north or Ho Chi Minh City in the south. Many people from Vietnam have **emigrated** to other countries. There are about 1.25 million **immigrants** from Vietnam in the United States! What is their home country like? Read ahead to find out!

The board game *xiangqi* originated in China, but is popular throughout Vietnam.

Han Hanh Gap Ong!

Meeting a new friend is always exciting. Someone from Vietnam might smile and say, *"Han hanh gap ong!"* That means "Pleased to meet you!"

Vietnamese is a **tonal language** like many others in Asia. How you say a word can change its meaning. Even changing a syllable in the word can change its meaning. Vietnamese has six different tones for

Greetings in Vietnam depend on who you're addressing.

saying a word. Words can be said louder or quieter. They can be said harder or softer. Or longer or shorter. Any of these tones can give words completely different meanings.

Which tone is used depends on a number of things. How old is the person they're speaking to? How well do they know the person? Is the person a man or a woman? Is the person single or married? An older man should be greeted with *"Chao ong."* An older woman would be greeted with *"Chao chi."* If that older woman is your grandmother, you would say *"Chao ba."*

Cao Dai is the third largest religion in Vietnam.

Following Cao Dai

See that giant eye painted on the wall? It's looking right at you! It might seem a little scary. But Vietnamese people know this is the Divine Eye. It is a symbol of a religion known as *Cao Dai*. The eye is not there to be frightening. It is there to watch over you.

Cao Dai means "high palace" or the "kingdom of heaven." The faith is a blend of different beliefs. Followers believe in a

Cao Dai temples are very ornate and colorful.

god that is a combination of different faiths. They want to bring the world's religions together and make them one.

    The Vietnamese people often mix religious beliefs. Some believe the teachings of a Chinese man named Confucius. Others follow the lessons of an Indian prince named Buddha. Still others are Catholic or Protestant and pray to Jesus. Many blend all of these beliefs together.

Some of the best food in Vietnam is found, and enjoyed, on the street.

Pho and Street Food

Have you ever seen a food cart? They are found on city sidewalks and in parking lots. Sometimes these carts have the best food. This is true in Vietnam. Street food is popular and affordable. Customers order their food. Then they sit down on plastic stools to enjoy it.

Since the ocean is so close, a lot of seafood is served. *Pho*, or soup, is found everywhere. It is usually made with seafood

Durian has a sweet and savory taste.

or other meat. It will have noodles or rice in it. The Vietnamese like strong flavors. They often add spices like ginger, lime, cinnamon, or **coriander** to their food.

Some of the fruits found in the markets might look strange to you. **Durian** looks like a bumpy alien egg. Opened up, it looks like a pile of scrambled eggs. Other unusual fruit includes dragon fruit and **custard apples**.

Think!

A favorite Vietnamese dish is called *banh xeo*, or rice pancakes. Often they are filled with meat, such as **prawns**. The yellow color comes from the spice **turmeric**. Do these pancakes remind you of other foods? How do they compare to Mexico's tacos or France's crepes?

Most motorbikes have at least two people on them.

Gia Dinh and Xe May

Engines rumble. Horns honk. People shout. Crossing the street can be tricky and scary. In Vietnam, the streets are always crowded. It seems like everyone has a motorbike, or *xe may*. There are too many of them to count!

The city parks in Vietnam are a wonderful place to gather. In one spot, people might be learning ballroom dancing. In another spot, chess games are being played. Under the

New Year in Vietnam is also called Tet.
It is the biggest celebration of the year.

trees, a radio plays loud music. People are exercising. The basketball courts are filled with players.

Family, or *gia dinh*, is very important to the Vietnamese. Families are often very close. Most holidays are spent together sharing meals.

Look!

The Lunar New Year falls in January or February in Vietnam. Houses are cleaned from top to bottom. All the bad luck is swept out. Families gather on New Year's Day. No one is supposed to have sad thoughts. It is a time for happiness! Red decorations are found everywhere. Red stands for good luck. Think about New Year's in the United States. How is it the same? How is it different?

GLOSSARY

coriander (KOR-ee-an-dur) powder made from crushed seeds and added to food for flavor

custard apples (KUHS-turd AP-uhlz) tropical fruit with a sweet yellow pulp

durian (DOOR-ee-uhn) a spiny tropical fruit with a creamy pulp

emigrated (EM-ih-grayt-id) left your home country to live in another country

immigrants (IM-ih-gruhnts) people who have moved from one country to another and settled there

prawns (PRAHNZ) sea creatures like large shrimp

tonal language (TOHN-uhl LANG-gwij) a language that uses tones to determine meaning

turmeric (TUR-mur-ik) a plant related to ginger, used to add flavor and color to dishes

Vietnamese Words

cao dai (COW DYE) high palace, kingdom of heaven

Chao ong/Chao chi/Chao ba (CHOW OHM/CHOW CHEE/CHOW BAH) Greetings

gia dinh (YA DIN) family

Han hanh gap ong (HAHNG HINE GUP OHM) Pleased to meet you

pho (FUH) soup

xe may (SAY MY) motorbike

FIND OUT MORE

BOOKS

Chu, Trina. *Escaping Vietnam: A Refugee's Tale.* Seattle: CreateSpace, 2016.

Labrie, Julia. *Cultural Traditions in Vietnam.* St. Catharines, ON: Crabtree Publishing Co., 2018.

Lai, Thanhha. *Inside Out and Back Again.* New York: HarperCollins, 2011.

Murray, Stuart. *Vietnam War.* New York: DK Eyewitness Books, 2017.

WEBSITES

Easy Science for Kids—Vietnam
http://easyscienceforkids.com/all-about-vietnam/
Read fun facts and learn some vocabulary.

National Geographic Kids—Vietnam
http://kids.nationalgeographic.com/explore/countries/vietnam/#vietnam-ha-long-bay.jpg
Learn about Vietnam's people, geography, language, and more.

Science Kids—Country Facts
www.sciencekids.co.nz/sciencefacts/countries/vietnam.html
Try some activities and check out more interesting information about Vietnam.

INDEX

C
Cao Dai, 10–13
cities, 4, 5

D
Divine Eye, 11

F
food, 14–17

G
games, 6

H
Hanoi, 5
Ho Chi Minh City, 5
Hoi An, 4
holidays, 20–21

I
immigrants, 5

L
language, 7–9

M
motorbikes, 18–19

N
New Year, 20, 21

P
parks, 19, 21
pho, 15, 17

R
religion, 10–13

S
street food, 14, 15

T
Tet, 20
tonal language, 7, 9
transportation, 18–19

V
Vietnam
    population, 5
    size, 5

X
xiangqi, 6

ABOUT THE AUTHOR

Tamra Orr is the author of hundreds of books for readers of all ages. She graduated from Ball State University, but moved with her husband and four children to Oregon in 2001. She is a full-time author, and when she isn't researching and writing, she writes letters to friends all over the world. Orr enjoys life in the big city of Portland and feels very lucky to be surrounded by so much diversity.

RECEIVED NOV 1 4 2018